CAMPFIRE

This is a work of fiction. All of the characters, events, and organizations portrayed in this work are either products of the authors' imagination or used fictitiously.

Campfire

Copyright © 2016 by Joseph Zettelmaier

ISBN-13: 978-1944540494

For information about production rights, visit:
www.jzettelmaier.com

Published by Sordelet Ink
WWW.SORDELETINK.COM

CAMPFIRE

A PLAY BY
JOSEPH ZETTELMAIER

SORDELET
ink

CAMPFIRE premiered on October 7, 2016 at the Ringwald Theatre (Ferndale, MI). It was directed by Brandy Joe Plambeck. Scenic and Property Design by Jennifer Maiseloff. Costume Design by Vince Kelley. Sound & Lighting Design by Brandy Joe Plambeck. Fight Choreography by Jonathan Davidson. Property Assistance by Andy Gaitens. Stage Managed by Megan Paruta. The cast was as follows:

MARCUS: Joel Mitchell
KAT: Julia Garlotte
JOHNNY: Eric Eilersen
MAYA: Allison Megroet

For information about production rights,
visit www.jzettelmaier.com.

Cast of Characters

MARCUS - 50s (ALSO PLAYS GEORGE & CARL)
KAT - 30s (ALSO PLAYS ETTA & GIRL)
JOHNNY - 20s (ALSO PLAYS JAKOB & BOY, VOICES BENJAMIN)
MAYA - 20s (ALSO PLAYS CAROLYN & JENNY)

(Lights up. A bonfire in the woods. MARCUS is stoking the fire, throwing in kindling, while humming a song to himself. After a bit, KAT enters)

MARCUS
Yeah?

KAT
He's almost here.

MARCUS
"Almost" can mean anything. Are we talkin' an hour? Two hours?

KAT
Verbatim - "I'm almost there."

MARCUS
And you didn't ask him to elaborate?

KAT
Am I his social secretary? He'll get here when he gets here.

MARCUS
Jesus, girl. What's chompin' on your ass?

KAT
I...why do you have to ask it like that?

(Beat)

MARCUS
I'm grizzled?

(She laughs. He motions for her to sit next to him. She does. She kicks at the fire)

MARCUS
Stop that.

KAT
No. *(She kicks at the fire again)*

MARCUS
I got that set up perfectly. Stop kicking it.

KAT
I wanna kick something.

MARCUS
Kick Johnny when he gets here. Leave my fire out of it.

KAT
I'm stoking it. With my foot.

MARCUS
Honey, that's my job. This beauty's gonna last us a good two, three hours easy. Leave it be.

KAT
This is a good night for it.

MARCUS
Yep.

KAT
Cold, but not freezing. Smells like autumn.

MARCUS
It is autumn.

KAT
Hence, the smell. *(She gets up, moves around)*

MARCUS
You miss him.

KAT
Johnny?

MARCUS
Not Johnny.

KAT
Oh. I mean…yeah. OK. I miss him.

MARCUS
Totally natural.

KAT
I know that, Marcus. People die and you miss them. This isn't new information.

MARCUS
I'm just saying…?

KAT
What? Are you gonna spin some folksy wisdom passed down from your grandpappy?

MARCUS
I liked you better when you were little.

(KAT laughs a little)

MARCUS
Swear to god. Back when you were in pigtails,

you didn't bust my chops all the time.

KAT
Yes, I did.

MARCUS
Yeah, well, you were cute then so you could get away with it.

KAT
You're saying I'm not cute now.

MARCUS
There. Right there. That's you busting my chops.

(She sits next to him. He puts his arm around her)

MARCUS
I miss him too.

KAT
You guys fought all the time.

MARCUS
Brothers fight. So do brothers and sisters. Doesn't mean you don't love 'em through it all.

(She stares into the fire)

KAT
Did I let dad down?

MARCUS
No. Don't ever think that.

KAT
You saw the way he was looking at me when...

MARCUS
Kat, he loved you. No matter what else, he loved you.

KAT
It's a big "what else," Uncle Marcus.

MARCUS
You get too hung up on that. Always have.

KAT
I should've married Cody.

MARCUS
No. Oh god no.

KAT
He asked. Twice.

MARCUS
Cody Stubbs was an idiot. And a drunk. A drunk
idiot.

KAT
I'd have a kid by now. That's all I'm saying.

MARCUS
Your dad didn't want you to grab the first comer,
just to swell the ranks. The Carver name means
something.

KAT
I know. I feel like I have that tattooed under my
eyelids.

(Beat)

MARCUS
So that's what's chompin' on your ass.

KAT
There's got to be a better way to say that.

MARCUS
You think your dad died angry 'cause you didn't

give him a grandbaby?

(She shrugs)

MARCUS
Katrina...

KAT
You don't get it. I mean, I'm not getting any younger.

MARCUS
There's time.

KAT
And it's down to me and Johnny, unless you have some secret love-child hidden somewhere.

MARCUS
That isn't funny.

(She stops)

KAT
I'm sorry. That...I wasn't thinking.

MARCUS
I know.

KAT
Sometimes I just get going and I don't...

MARCUS
It's all right.

KAT
I just...I know how much you wanted kids.

MARCUS
We're not gonna talk about that, ok? I love you like you're my own, but we're not gonna talk

about that.

KAT
Ok.

MARCUS
Ok.

(Silence. They watch the fire)

KAT
You really are grizzled.

(She smiles. He laughs a little)

MARCUS
You're too good at that.

KAT
At what?

MARCUS
Getting people to not be mad at you.

KAT
Years of practice. And necessity leading to that practice.

MARCUS
Mind if I ask?

KAT
Ask what?

MARCUS
Are you looking?

KAT
Looking for...? Oh. Oh god.

MARCUS
I know some nice fellas down at the farmers market.

KAT
No. No no no no no.

MARCUS
Clearly, it's been on your mind.

KAT
I have lots of things on my mind, all the time! And like 90% of them are things I don't want to talk about.

MARCUS
Look. I get how uncomfortable this is, but...

KAT
I know.

MARCUS
I don't mean to pressure. Really.

KAT
Can this wait til Johnny gets here to talk about this?

MARCUS
Sure.

(Beat)

MARCUS
Of course, that could be an hour, two hours...

KAT
Know what? I'll call him again.

MARCUS
Be careful out there.

KAT
I always am.

MARCUS
There's spoooooky things in the woods.

KAT
Ha ha ha.

(Just as she starts to go, JOHNNY leaps out of the darkness, roaring. KAT screams. MARCUS jumps up. JOHNNY immediately starts laughing at their reactions)

JOHNNY
...oh man...so good...sooooo good...

KAT
Asshole! *(She slugs him in the arm)*

JOHNNY
...Your faces...oh man...one of you must've shit yourself....

(She slugs him again)

MARCUS
Maybe your sister.

KAT
Hey! *(She slugs MARCUS)*

MARCUS
Ow! Damn, you got a bony hand!

(JOHNNY grabs KAT in a hug, swings her around)

KAT
Whoa!

JOHNNY
Sistersistersistersistersistersistersister...

KAT
Let me down, you dillweed!

(He sets her down)

JOHNNY
Miss me?

KAT
With every shot.

(JOHNNY kisses her forehead roughly)

JOHNNY
Uncle Marcus!

MARCUS
C'mere, boy.

(They hug)

MARCUS
Goddamn, it's been too long.

JOHNNY
I know, I know.

MARCUS
Is there a wall around Denver? Are you physically incapable of visiting?

JOHNNY
I was here last year, for...

(Beat. An awkward silence)

JOHNNY
Shit. I just made things weird.

KAT
You're such an ass.

JOHNNY
I wasn't thinking! I'm sorry!

MARCUS
It's all right. How's school treating you?

KAT
...he said, changing the subject.

JOHNNY
You know. Fine. Long.

KAT
You're never going to graduate.

JOHNNY
I'm getting a Masters. These things take time!

MARCUS
She's proud of you. We both are.

JOHNNY
And I figure if I wait it out long enough, that whole Debt-Forgiveness thing will eventually kick in.

KAT
Suddenly less proud.

JOHNNY
Damn, it's good to be back! Look at this place! Just like when we were kids!

KAT
Right?

JOHNNY
So cool. Tell me our treehouse is still....

KAT
Nope.

JOHNNY
Dammit. Really?

MARCUS
That snow storm this year? The big one? Whole tree came down.

JOHNNY
Well, nothing lasts forever, I guess.

KAT
Some things do. Just not that tree.

(As they've talked, MAYA has slowly entered to the edge of the campfire light)

MARCUS
Hey! Who the hell...?

(MARCUS' hand goes to the knife on his belt. KAT jumps)

KAT
Oh my god!

JOHNNY
Wait! Slow down! This is...hold on a sec...Maya? Baby?

(MAYA enters the light, goes to JOHNNY)

JOHNNY
Uncle Marcus, Kat...this is Maya.

MAYA
Hello.

(They just stare at her. She clears her throat, thinking they didn't hear her)

MAYA
He..hello?

JOHNNY
Maya is my girlfriend.

MARCUS
You have a girlfriend?

JOHNNY
I do.

MAYA
And it's me.

(MARCUS goes to her)

MARCUS
I'm sorry, girl. We're not...Johnny didn't say anything. *(Offers his hand)* Marcus Carver. It's a pleasure.

(She hugs him)

MARCUS
Oh!

JOHNNY
Yeah, she's a hugger.

MAYA
It's just, Johnny's told me so much about you both.

KAT
Really?

MAYA
And you're his big sister? Kat?

KAT
I don't understand anything that's happening right now.

JOHNNY
I just thought it was time you all met.

MARCUS
How long have you two been together?

MAYA
Almost a year now.

JOHNNY
I guess since right after...

MAYA
We're both in the Creative Writing program. We've known each other for a while, and just...

JOHNNY
Honey, they don't need to know the whole...

MAYA
No, it's so romantic! We both ran with the same group, but we never really talked, you know? I had such a crush on him, but I'm kind of old fashioned, I guess? I just kept waiting and waiting for him to ask me out and he never did.

JOHNNY
I never did.

MAYA
So finally, finally, he comes back from his...um...

JOHNNY
From Dad's funeral.

MAYA
And I get this knock on my door. Middle of the night. Scared the pants off me. I open the door, and there's Johnny, just soaked. It was raining. I should've said that. He looked like he was in a John Cusack movie. And he just grabbed me....

JOHNNY
Ok.

MAYA
...and kissed me. Here's this guy I've been, like, pining over for two years, we've barely ever spoken, and...wow. It was so romantic. And we've been together ever since.

(Beat)

KAT
What the hell is going on?

MARCUS
We don't mean to be rude, Maya. Really. We just thought it would be the three of us.

MAYA
I know. I'm so so sorry. I didn't mean to intrude, it's just...

MARCUS
Really, It's fine.

MAYA
...Johnny told me. About your tradition. And I knew I wanted to see it, you know? I wanted to be a part of it.

MARCUS
How's that?

JOHNNY
I told her about the campfires.

KAT
Awesome.

MAYA
The whole family getting together, telling stories around a campfire. That's so great. And when Johnny said you guys were getting together,

honoring his dad, I begged him to let me come.

JOHNNY
I wanted to surprise you. I thought it would be
fun.

KAT
Classic Johnny.

MAYA
My thesis is actually about American Oral Tradition.
I just...*(Sensing the emotion of the group)* We
should have said something first. I'm so sorry.

MARCUS
It's fine.

JOHNNY
See?

KAT
It's just...this is about our dad.

MAYA
I know. I'm sorry.

KAT
You didn't know him.

JOHNNY
Kat!

KAT
I don't mean that to be cruel, but can you see
why, from our standpoint, it's weird?

MAYA
I can. I do. This was a bad idea.

JOHNNY
Wait. Stop. This isn't...Kat, what are you doing?

KAT
Expressing myself in a clear and honest fashion?

JOHNNY
This is my girlfriend. I love her. I wanted her to be with me tonight, and I wanted you to meet her. She's important to me. So I need you to be cool with this.

(Beat)

MARCUS
It's fine by me. Really.

JOHNNY
Kat.

(KAT looks to JOHNNY, gauges his sincerity)

KAT
You love her?

JOHNNY
Yeah.

KAT
And you love him?

MAYA
I do.

KAT
Ok. Yeah, ok. Welcome aboard.

MAYA
(Hugging KAT) Thank you! I can't tell you what that means to me.

KAT
It's fine.

MAYA
I know how close you two are and...thank you.
Thank you both.

MARCUS
You're a real sweetheart, aren't you?

MAYA
Oh. I don't...am I?

JOHNNY
You are.

(MARCUS tosses her a beer)

MARCUS
Good hands too.

MAYA
Would you believe this isn't the first beer I've
caught?

MARCUS
I would believe that.

KAT
What am I? The Queen of...like...beerless land?

JOHNNY
Wow.

KAT
Shut up.

(MARCUS throws KAT a beer)

KAT
There we go.

MARCUS
Johnny? You twenty-one yet?

JOHNNY
I'm twenty-five!

MARCUS
Christ, really?

KAT
You gave him his first beer when he was fifteen.

MARCUS
I did?

KAT
4th of July. Lake Eleanor.

MARCUS
Huh. Sounds like something I would do. *(Tosses JOHNNY a beer)* So Maya...how much did Johnny tell you about our campfires?

MAYA
That they're a Carver family tradition. That the family always gets together for big events and tells stories.

KAT
It's more than that.

MAYA
I'm sure.

KAT
The stories, I mean. They're...

MARCUS
Kat, stop scaring the girl.

KAT
What? I just...

MARCUS
The stories we share...some of 'em have been in

our family since before the Revolutionary War. Some are just crazy yarns we make up 'cause... well, 'cause it's funny as hell. Depends on the time of year, depends on the situation. But each and every Carver is a born storyteller.

MAYA
I can tell.

JOHNNY
It's why you love me.

MARCUS
But there's something I wanna make clear. You've got your paper on folklore and whatnot, yeah?

MAYA
Yeah.

MARCUS
These stories aren't for that. They're for us. If you're in the circle, around this fire, you can hear these stories. But only tonight, and only us. All right?

MAYA
I won't write anything down. I promise.

MARCUS
Johnny inviting you here...that's important. He wouldn't have done so unless he knew you were something special.

(JOHNNY takes her hand)

JOHNNY
It's true.

MARCUS
It was a surprise to see you here, sure, but not

an unpleasant one, Maya. The Carver Circle is getting too small, and I'm getting too old. It's damn fine to see a new face in the fire light.

MAYA
Thank you.

KAT
I think you should start, Marcus.

MARCUS
Well, I have had the most beer.

(They laugh)

MAYA
What kind of stories do you tell?

MARCUS
Like I said, depends on why we're gathering and when. Tonight, we honor my brother Mitchell, who died one year ago today.

(They raise their beers)

MARCUS
He is survived by his brother Marcus, and his children John and Katrina. Autumn was always Mitchell's favorite time of year. This land belonged to my brother, and then it came to me. Autumn is the harvest. It's cider and woodsmoke and long nights. We bring in our crops, and we have a chance to celebrate one more time before winter sets in. We will not mourn Mitchell's passing tonight. Instead, we're going to celebrate the way Carvers have celebrated since god knows when.

(KAT and JOHNNY smile, excited)

KAT
Scary stories?

MARCUS
Well, what do you think?

(She laughs. MAYA leans against JOHNNY, who puts his arm around her)

MARCUS
How about it, Maya? You wanna hear a scary story?

MAYA
Yes, sir.

MARCUS
Well, all right then.

(The lights dim to just the fire. The scene changes behind them)

MARCUS
Now this one...this is an old one. Back in the days when America wasn't more than a newborn. This land looked real different back then. Wide open fields, deep forests and hardly a soul to be found.

JOHNNY
It's important to set the feel of the story, you know? So you can picture...

(MARCUS glares at him. JOHNNY falls silent, motions MARCUS to continue)

MARCUS
In those days, the 1700s, a man could settle this land without the government getting its hands all over it. He could build himself a cabin, down by

a stream, made from wood he cut down with his own two hands. That's just what Jakob did.

(Lights begin to reveal the interior of an old cabin. JOHNNY takes on the role of Jakob. He throws logs into a fire as MARCUS talks)

MARCUS
Jakob Van Dorn was a man who'd seen too much of the world. He was a Dutch settler who fought in the French & Indian War. But the war cost him, as I suppose they always do. Not a leg, or an arm. No, Jakob's body made it through the battlefield with a few scars and nothing more. But Jakob's soul...

(JAKOB sits, stares at an empty rocking chair)

MARCUS
It's a hard thing to lose a brother. One of the hardest things there is. Jakob watched his own get cut down before his very eyes. They say Jonas Van Dorn fell fighting a Mohawk. The French gave him a bullet, but it was the Mohawk that did him in. A man doesn't live long without a scalp.

(MARCUS draws his finger across his scalp. MAYA gasps)

MARCUS
Jakob was a broken man from that day forward. He'd loved Jonas dearly, and swore to his family that he'd look after him when they came over the sea. Jakob knew, he knew that he'd failed his kin in a way that went beyond forgiving. So the young soldier built himself a place in the woods, by a stream, where he'd never have to look another man in the eye, and see his own shame reflected

back at him. At least, that's what he'd hoped.

(A knock at the door of the cabin. JAKOB rises, grabs a gun)

JAKOB
Who's there?

(No answer. A knock again)

JAKOB
I've got a musket aimed at the door. I'll put a hole through it and you unless you give me your name.

(No response at all. JAKOB stares at the door, confused. After a beat, he opens it. An unconscious woman lies at the doorstep. ETTA is played by KAT)

JAKOB
Christ Almighty...

(JAKOB sets his gun down and picks ETTA up. She moans. He is about to set her in the rocking chair, then puts her in his own chair instead. He gets her some water)

JAKOB
What's this then? You live?

(She coughs while drinking)

JAKOB
You live.

(She takes a deep breath. He lifts her face)

JAKOB
Water's for drinking, not for breathing.

ETTA
...give me....a moment...

JAKOB
I'll even give you two.

(ETTA manages to compose herself)

JAKOB
Have you et?

(She stares, unsure and exhausted)

JAKOB
Food. Bread, meat and the like.

ETTA
Not in a while, no.

(He goes to the pantry. He returns with bread and an apple)

JAKOB
Keep these down, and we'll see about more.

(She tears into the food)

JAKOB
Who are you?

(She looks up)

JAKOB
A name.

ETTA
Etta.

JAKOB
Why are you here, Etta?

ETTA
All depends.

JAKOB
On what?

ETTA
On if you're Jakob Van Dorn.

(Beat)

JAKOB
And if I am?

(She rises, suddenly a bit manic)

ETTA
You are. I know you are. I was told where to find you.

JAKOB
Don't nobody know I'm here.

ETTA
You would think that...of course, but... *(She sees the rocking chair, stops)* You still have it.

JAKOB
Have what?

ETTA
His chair. *(She goes to it, touches it)* He made this, with his own two hands. I can tell. I can feel it...

(JAKOB grabs her roughly, pushing her away from the chair)

JAKOB
I don't know you. I don't know what this is, but touch that chair again and I'll gut you.

ETTA
I never meant...

JAKOB
Who are you?

ETTA
I told you. My name is Etta.

(JAKOB grabs her, slams her into a wall)

JAKOB
Why are you here?!

ETTA
For your brother! For Jonas!

(He releases her)

JAKOB
Jonas is dead. Dead now for a year.

ETTA
I know.

JAKOB
Then you made this journey for nothing.

ETTA
You misunderstand.

JAKOB
Get out.

ETTA
I'm not looking for Jonas.

JAKOB
I said out!

ETTA
I'm here on his behalf.

(Beat)

JAKOB
He didn't know you.

ETTA
Well...

JAKOB
We were never apart. I knew everyone he knew.

ETTA
You're apart now.

JAKOB
(Going to the door) Get out.

ETTA
I can't leave.

JAKOB
I'll give you a kick to get you started.

ETTA
Please! I've travelled far! From Fort Edward!

JAKOB
Don't speak to me of that place.

ETTA
I must. I have to.

JAKOB
I lost everything at Bloody Pond. Don't... *(He grabs his musket, points it at her)* Leave now or die now.

ETTA
I wouldn't be the only dead one here.

JAKOB
I remember you. Heard of you. You're a madwoman.

ETTA
I've been so called.

JAKOB
The madwoman. From outside the fort. The woman who lives in the woods.

ETTA
You live in the woods.

JAKOB
I'm not mad. I don't lie with Indians.

ETTA
Don't...

JAKOB
I've heard what they say. You bedded with the Shawnee, yes? Had a child with a savage.

ETTA
That does not matter.

JAKOB
Take your sickness out of my house. Bother some-one else.

ETTA
He won't let me!

(He lowers his gun, startled by her outburst)

ETTA
Every day! He has been with me every day since... pushing me! Pushing me towards you! I had to find you, or he would not stop shouting! He... Jakob, he couldn't find you! He was lost and I... they left his body on the battlefield. Left it there, bleeding and...the Mohawk took his scalp. That's how it happens. A warrior dies, lost in battle, his honor taken from him, and he rises up. His spirit wanders until it finds someone. *(She moves behind*

the chair) Choo-noo-khoo. You know what that is?

JAKOB
A scalped man.

ETTA
The spirit of the scalped man. It cannot rest until it goes home. But Jonas has no home, and he has come to live... *(She taps her head)* Here.

JAKOB
I don't believe in Indian legends.

ETTA
I dug through the corpses after the battle, like a crow. That's how he found me. Grabbed on to me and won't let go. Every day he whispers into my ears, tells me to find you. But Jakob van Dorn is not an easy man to find.

JAKOB
You're lying. You're sick in your head.

ETTA
He wants to know why you ran.

JAKOB
What?

ETTA
You said you would watch over him, but you ran.

(The candles in the cabin begin to flicker)

ETTA
Gunfire. The war cries of the Mohawk and the Iroquois. You and Jonas were scouts. Just scouts. But Major Lyman put rifles in your hands and ordered you to fight. In all his life, Jonas was never so scared.

JAKOB
Stop.

ETTA
The man who cut him down...Jonas froze when
he saw him. Taller than him by a head, covered in
deer skin and blood. A musket ball dropped your
brother, and as he fell to the ground, he saw you
running. War had your blood running yellow, and
you ran. He was watching you when the Mohawk
grabbed his head and...

JAKOB
STOP! Stop, god damn you! (Pulls a knife and
goes after her. She dodges him, still ranting)

ETTA
He didn't even know he was dead until he found
me, going through his corpse's pockets. I wear
him like a pelt now, and I hear his every word.
"Why did you leave me, Jakob? Why?"

JAKOB
(Collapsing in despair) You couldn't...these things
aren't real.

ETTA
A man may not understand a thing, yet that thing
exists all the same.

JAKOB
I loved him.

ETTA
I know.

JAKOB
My brother, my only friend and I...

ETTA
Tell him. Tell him the truth.

(Beat. JAKOB looks at ETTA)

JAKOB
There is a shadow at your shoulder, but it isn't yours.

ETTA
He is here with us.

JAKOB
Now?

ETTA
Always.

JAKOB
Jonas...my brother.

ETTA
Speak to him. Free yourself. Free him.

JAKOB
There can be no forgiveness for me. What I did to you...there is no sin greater. *(He leans against the wall, his emotions overtaking him)* We were woodsmen, Jonas. Not soldiers. We thought the war would bring us excitement, cool our blood. You were braver than I. Five years younger, but more a man than I ever was. I saw you on the field, fighting rifle and axe. And I knew, I knew in my heart that I could not protect you. All I could hope to do was protect myself. The man in front of us was torn apart by grapeshot and it could have been me. It very nearly was me. A man turned into bloody pieces fit for no more than a hog's trough. I didn't even realize I was running

until I was within the trees again. I turned to find you and... *(He weeps)* Gone. I could not see you among so many dead. We were going to make our fortune on the rivers, marry plump wives and live off the land...and it was all taken from us because we were fool enough to think we should fight. I failed you. You, who I held above all others, and I let you die. It should have been me.

ETTA
Again.

(He stares at her)

JAKOB
It should have been me.

ETTA
Yes.

(ETTA drops limp to the ground. After a beat, JAKOB goes to her. She slowly comes to)

ETTA
Yes. That did it.

JAKOB
Did what?

ETTA
The choo-noo-khoo rides me no more. HA! Free! Free of your cursed brother!

JAKOB
Don't call him that.

ETTA
You must have felt as I felt, carrying that braying ass with you everywhere you went.

(He pulls his knife, points it at her)

JAKOB
Woman, I will cut your tongue out before I hear you say that again.

(She rises, backs away)

ETTA
You know I'm right. I have lived with him only a year, but you bore him for a lifetime. "I miss my brother, find me my brother." Enough to make me retch.

(He grabs her, throws her into a wall)

JAKOB
You come here, make me relive that day...that alone is enough for me to kill you.

(ETTA spits in his face. He lets her go)

ETTA
Perhaps. But I know something about you, boy. You are and always will be a coward.

(He simply stares at her, the truth of it hitting him)

ETTA
You Van Dorns. You've given me more trouble the last few months than I've suffered in years. Keep your little shack, tucked away where no one will find you. I hope you die here, alone with your misery. You deserve no better.

(He grips his knife tight but does nothing)

ETTA
Craven. Pathetic. A mincing, mewling...

(He finally snaps. He charges her and stabs her

repeatedly. She drops)

JAKOB
A quieter tongue would've given you a longer
life.

*(A wind picks up in the cabin. The lights flicker
again. JAKOB grabs his rifle, spinning around.
Suddenly, the wind stops and very little light is
left in the room. Slowly, the rocking chair begins to
rock of its own accord)*

JAKOB
What in god's name…

(The chair begins to rock more)

JAKOB
…Jonas?

(The chair begins to rock faster)

JAKOB
No. No no no no no.

(The chair rocks wildly)

JAKOB
She said you were gone! That you were free! (He
goes to the chair, kneels at it) Jonas! Please! I
don't know how to help you! I would take your
place if I could, but I cannot! Just tell me what
you want!

*(ETTA suddenly lurches up. She is still dead,
though JONAS speaks through her)*

ETTA
Jakob.

(JAKOB turns to her, grabbing his musket. He fires

and ETTA drops. She suddenly jerks back up again)

ETTA
Brother.

JAKOB
Oh god...Jonas?

ETTA
Brother?

(JAKOB goes to him)

JAKOB
I am here. Jonas, I am here.

ETTA
I cannot see you.

JAKOB
I am next to you.

ETTA
You can hear me?

JAKOB
I can.

ETTA
I forgive you.

(Beat)

JAKOB
What?

ETTA
I know why you ran. I heard all that you said. And I forgive you.

JAKOB
Jonas, why are you here? Why can't you rest?

(Beat)

ETTA
I miss you.

JAKOB
And I, you.

ETTA
Then join me.

(Beat)

JAKOB
What?

ETTA
We are brothers. We have always been by the other's side. It is wrong that we are separated now.

JAKOB
But I still live.

ETTA
A coward's life. Hidden in these woods, hidden from your shame.

JAKOB
I know.

ETTA
Then join me.

(ETTA goes limp in his arms)

JAKOB
Jonas?

(No answer at first. Then, the chair begins to rock slowly)

JAKOB
I know what you want, but…I am afraid.

(The chair continues to rock. JAKOB takes a long breath)

JAKOB
And I am tired of being afraid.

(JAKOB takes the knife, and sits in the chair. He is very scared, but finds his resolve)

JAKOB
I'm coming, Jonas.

(JAKOB takes the knife and draws it across his hairline. Blood pours out and he screams)

JAKOB
I'm coming!

(He begins to pull his own scalp off as lights fade, returning to the campfire. The light only reveals MARCUS & MAYA, as KAT and JOHNNY rejoin when they've resumed their roles)

MARCUS
They say that Jakob laid there for days before anyone stumbled on the cabin. Said there was a whole flock of crows on the roof, waiting to get in and pick the body bare.

MAYA
Murder. It's a murder of crows.

MARCUS
Right. That's right.

MAYA
Sorry, I didn't mean to interrupt.

MARCUS
When they finally broke down his door, there he was...sitting in Jonas' chair, with his own bloody scalp hanging from his fingertips.

MAYA
Wow. Just...wow.

MARCUS
Here. *(He tosses her another beer)*

MAYA
Thanks.

MARCUS
My great grampa told that one to me and my brother when we were...I must've been six, so Mitch would've been eight.

MAYA
That's a really intense story for a six-year-old.

MARCUS
I loved it. Always loved the scary ones.

MAYA
I was the same way.

MARCUS
Is that a fact?

MAYA
When I was little, really little, my dad took me to see one of the Nightmare on Elm Street movies. I was way too young for it, but somehow he got me in and I loved it. I don't know how he knew it, but he knew I'd love it.

MARCUS
Fathers know their daughters.

(KAT & JOHNNY have returned)

KAT
I can't believe you said that with a straight face.

JOHNNY
Come on, Kat.

KAT
I hate those kind of blanket statements! "Fathers know their daughters." Really, Marcus? You really think…

MARCUS
I didn't mean anything by it.

(Beat)

KAT
I know.

MAYA
Are you ok?

(KAT stares at MAYA, caught off guard by the question)

KAT
Yes?

JOHNNY
This is why we used to call her "Little Mary Stormcloud."

KAT
Excuse me?

JOHNNY
What? You knew we called you that.

KAT
Why are you telling her that?

JOHNNY
She's my girlfriend. I tell her lots of stuff.

KAT
(Turning to MAYA) So, like, do you have this picture of who I am, cobbled together from the stuff Johnny's told you?

MAYA
No.

KAT
Because I'm feeling a little judged.

MARCUS
Kat...

KAT
I'm sorry! There's this...I thought we were all going to get together and bond and now my guard's all up because... *(She trails off)*

MAYA
Because I'm here.

KAT
That was shitty. I didn't mean to say it like that.

MAYA
But it's true. I'm intruding.

JOHNNY
No. Absolutely not. By definition, intruders aren't invited, and I invited you.

MARCUS
Kat, you remember the first time you brought Cody over to meet the family?

KAT
Ok. That's not even the same thing.

MARCUS
Really?

KAT
It wasn't at a campfire!

JOHNNY
No, but it was Thanksgiving.

KAT
Not the same thing!

MARCUS
Remember how well he and your old man got along?

KAT
Dad loved Cody!

(MARCUS and JOHNNY laugh)

KAT
I...they went fishing together!

MARCUS
Your dad damn near tied a cinder block 'round his neck and pushed him in.

JOHNNY
Dad hated Cody, Kat. That special kind of hate fathers reserve for drunken assbags who crash their daughters' pick-up.

KAT
Why did I not know this?

MARCUS
Why do you think? You loved Cody.

KAT
That's maybe a stronger word than I'd use.

MARCUS
Well, you cared enough to keep him around for a while. Mitch did his best to support that. But I'll tell you this for true; when you finally kicked Cody to the curb, your dad busted out the special cider.

KAT
Really?

JOHNNY
We got tore up that night. Tore up but good.

MARCUS
I don't get drunk easy, but...

KAT
But Dad was always telling me...

MARCUS
Any father wants to see his children end up with someone, someone that'll make them happy. So he put on a good face.

KAT
But Cody didn't make me happy.

JOHNNY
Took you long enough to figure it out.

MARCUS
All that matters is that you did figure it out.

(KAT is silent, absorbing this. Beat)

JOHNNY
Oh my god, I'm starving! Are you guys starving?

MARCUS
I could eat.

JOHNNY
I'm gonna go find us some s'mores or wieners or something.

KAT
Really? Wieners?

JOHNNY
Grow up.

KAT
They call them "hot dogs" now.

JOHNNY
Uncle Marcus, you have any food in this place?

MARCUS
It's a farm. There's food.

JOHNNY
Come on. Let's grab some stuff.

MAYA
I'll help. *(She stands)*

(JOHNNY stops her)

JOHNNY
We got this. Why don't you and Kat just stay put, keep the fire going?

(KAT glares at him)

MAYA
Oh. Um...ok.

KAT
For Christ's sake...

MARCUS
Yeah. I'll show you where I keep the food.

JOHNNY
Good. Excellent. Let's go.

MARCUS
(Looking at them) You two have fun. *(He and JOHNNY walk off)*

MAYA
This is Johnny trying to force us to talk, isn't it?

KAT
Smart and pretty.

MAYA
You think I'm pretty?

KAT
Yeah. You're way out of his league.

MAYA
That's...come on.

KAT
It's true. You're an 8 easy, maybe even a 9 on a good day. And I get the vibe like you're smart.

MAYA
Thank you?

KAT
You get that you can do better than Johnny Carver, right?

MAYA
I love Johnny.

KAT
Why?

MAYA
What do you mean?

KAT
I've known my brother a long time. Obviously.
And I love him, but he's an idiot.

MAYA
He's not, though. He's...can we not do this?

KAT
Do what?

MAYA
Sit here and talk about boys. I feel a little...
middle-schooly.

KAT
Normally, yes. That would be totally fine with
me. But...look, Johnny bringing you here. That's
a big thing.

MAYA
I get that.

KAT
Right, except I think you don't. The Carvers....
were one of those families like....we take time.
We like to get to know people. You guys have
been together for almost a year, yeah?

MAYA
That's right.

KAT
Ok. That's the part that weirds me out. Until
today, Uncle Marcus and I didn't even know you
existed.

MAYA
We've kind of been in our own little bubble. You
know how it is, when you're just so into each other.

KAT
I'll take your word for it.

MAYA
You've never had that?

(Beat)

KAT
We're not here to talk about me.

MAYA
I'm sorry if I've pissed you off, but...no. No, I'm not sorry.

KAT
What?

MAYA
I haven't done anything wrong. Johnny asked me to be here; I'm here. He did his best to explain how important these campfires are. I'm trying to honor that. So whatever's pissing you off, it isn't me.

(KAT just stares at MAYA)

KAT
You pickin' a fight with me?

MAYA
No. Because you'd beat me up. I'm really confident about that.

KAT
(Laughing) You got no problem speaking your mind, do you?

MAYA
I'm a talker. I'm a hugger and a talker.

KAT
Ok. I can respect that. The talking, not the
hugging. You have any brothers or sisters?

MAYA
Only child.

KAT
I envy you. I really do.

(MAYA laughs at that)

KAT
What's your family like?

MAYA
Oh. Well, they live in Boulder. My dad's a mechanic,
my mom teaches second grade.

KAT
Mechanic, huh? He teach you anything?

MAYA
Sure. I helped him rebuild a 1971 Gremlin when
I was eighteen. I still drive it.

KAT
Oh god, I'm sorry to hear that. That is an ugly,
ugly vehicle.

MAYA
It grows on you. Like fungus. Or Johnny.

KAT
Dammit. See, you're doing that thing.

MAYA
What thing?

KAT
You're making me warm up to you.

MAYA
I know. I'm the worst.

KAT
You close with your folks?

MAYA
Very. I was...really sick for a while.

KAT
Oh. Shit, I'm sorry.

MAYA
It's ok. I beat it. But...

KAT
Can I ask? What it was, I mean.

(Beat)

MAYA
I don't really like to talk about it.

KAT
Fair enough.

MAYA
But...I don't know. When a family goes through something like that, it can make them all closer. I guess that's obvious, but...

KAT
It's good, though. Families should be close. One of the reasons Cody and I didn't work out. He got really jealous of the way I was with...well, with the two idiots getting wieners.

MAYA
Sounds like you could do better.

(KAT shrugs)

MAYA
You're really pretty.

KAT
I know.

MAYA
And modest.

KAT
(Chuckling) I lose patience with people who don't say what they think.

MAYA
Then we're going to get along just fine.

KAT
Yeah. Maybe.

MAYA
So…can I ask? You're single, then?

KAT
That…yes.

MAYA
We don't have to talk about it.

KAT
We sure don't. *(Drinks her beer)* You're pretty up on your old stories and legends, yeah?

MAYA
I know a lot of them, sure.

KAT
You ever hear the story of George Wixom's Wife?

MAYA
Maybe? Hum a few bars.

KAT

It's the one…ok. It's late 1800s, I think. Big city. Chicago or New York or something like that. This guy, George Wixom, he's a doctor, but he's more than a doctor. He's a scientist.

(The scene starts to change behind them. It becomes a well-furnished parlor and beside it, a dimly lit lab. A large cabinet is there)

KAT

Electricity was a big thing then. The new ways to use it, I mean. Traffic lights, phonographs, batteries…these were all brand new things. Hell, they'd just invented the telephone. Anyway, Dr. Wixom was tinkering around with all that shit. He was gonna be America's next big inventor. But then, there was his wife.

(MARCUS enters as George, a well-dressed, educated man. MAYA leaves as KAT speaks)

KAT

Her name was Carolyn, and she could've been his daughter, age-wise. He'd gotten her in the worst sort of way. There was no courtship, no romance. Her father basically sold her to Wixom, covering some sort of debt he owed. The doctor had always had an eye for the ladies, and Carolyn was a pretty one all right. But what he really wanted was a maid he didn't have to pay, a servant who wouldn't steal the silver. Those days, men could do whatever sick thing they wanted and what was a woman gonna do?

(George pours two glasses of brandy, checks his pocket watch)

KAT
What she did was fall in love with another man.
Wixom would take students from time to time,
teach them his trade. The student in question was
named Benjamin. He had been working with the
doctor for six months, and the minute he set eyes
on the doc's pretty caged bird, well it was all
over. The two started sneaking around when they
could, where they could. It was easy enough at
first, with the doctor spending half the day working in his basement. Of course, there wouldn't be
a story if their luck held out.

*(MAYA enters as Carolyn. She starts at the sight
of George)*

GEORGE
Hello, darling.

CAROLYN
George. *(She kisses him on the cheek)*

GEORGE
Where have you been?

CAROLYN
I was...the house was so stuffy today. I thought I
might get some air.

GEORGE
Late night for it. Late and cold.

CAROLYN
I like the autumn air. It's very...brisk.

(Uncomfortable silence. A large dog barks outside)

CAROLYN
Why don't I see to your supper? It sounds like
King is ready for the scraps.

GEORGE
Sit.

(She stares at him. He motions to the chair, with the second glass next to it)

GEORGE
Sit. Please.

(She does so)

GEORGE
A brandy, to warm you after your walk.

(She just stares at him)

GEORGE
Drink, god damn it!

(She jumps nervously, then takes a tentative drink)

GEORGE
Carolyn, what am I to do with you, hmm?

CAROLYN
I don't understand.

GEORGE
You don't understand. Funny, I said something similar today. I didn't understand why you would risk so much, after everything I've given you. A fine home to keep clean, fine dresses, even a fine mastiff to keep you company when I'm away.

CAROLYN
If I've done something to upset you...

GEORGE
Drink your drink and let me speak, or I'll snap your scrawny neck.

(She stops, terrified)

GEORGE
You are here to tend to my needs. Beyond that, I care very little about what you do. But infidelity, Carolyn? Even I have my limits.

(She's about to say something)

GEORGE
I would be very, very careful about saying anything at this moment.

(She remains silent)

GEORGE
Your little Benjamin came to me this afternoon. Told me the whole sordid business. I never suspected, Carolyn. Never! Marriage vows are a sacred thing and...anyway, my pupil is quite besotted with you. Even offered me a thousand dollars to end our marriage and set you free. Can you imagine the gall?

CAROLYN
What...what did he say?

GEORGE
Everything, dearest. Everything. Of course, I wouldn't hear of it. We are wed for life, you and I. A promise made to God.

CAROLYN
Please.

GEORGE
What's that?

CAROLYN
Please, I am begging you. Just let me go. I'll give

you anything you want, just...

GEORGE
You have nothing I want that I cannot simply take.

CAROLYN
Then I'll leave. I'll leave and never come back.

GEORGE
(Laughing, genuinely amused) You little twit, why on earth would you announce your intentions like that? Why not just sneak away? Christ.

CAROLYN
(Rising) Stop mocking me, you insufferable ass!

GEORGE
(Grabbing her roughly) Sit down, wife. You will want to hear how my meeting with your suitor ended.

CAROLYN
If you hurt him, I swear I'll...

(GEORGE strikes her. She falls into her chair)

GEORGE
You want to know if I hurt Benjamin. I did. I have.

CAROLYN
No!

GEORGE
But he still lives. Take comfort in that, whore.

CAROLYN
What did you do to him?!

GEORGE
Drugged him, firstly. He got more than he

expected in his liquor.

(She stares at her own glass)

GEORGE
Yours was merely brandy. I want you alert for what comes next.

CAROLYN
What does come next?

GEORGE
This. *(He goes to the cabinet. He's about to open it, then stops. He turns back to CAROLYN)* There's a little project I've been working on. Funny enough, Benjamin had been helping with it.

CAROLYN
You said he was...

GEORGE
Alive? He is, and he's helping me still.

CAROLYN
What do you mean?

GEORGE
The brain, my dear. It's the center of everything. Thought, instinct, emotion. The heart is a leathery muscle for pumping blood, nothing more. All that we are exists in the mind. But oftentimes, when the body suffers horrible injury, the brain suffers as well. Shock, stroke, meningitis, lesions...the list goes on. But what if there was a way to protect the brain from these sympathetic injuries? Some means of keeping it safe while the body repairs itself?

CAROLYN
George, what have you done?

(He opens the cabinet. Inside, a human skull floats in a jar of water. It retains its eyes, and wires are connected to it. CAROLYN gasps)

GEORGE
He's not as pretty as you remember, is he?

CAROLYN
No. Oh god no.

GEORGE
I'm not sure I've perfected the process yet...

CAROLYN
Benjamin!

GEORGE
...but sometimes, one has to roll the dice.

(She runs to the cabinet, but GEORGE catches her)

GEORGE
Careful now, dearest. He lives, but precariously.

CAROLYN
No, no, no...

GEORGE
He had some interesting physiological traits that made him an ideal subject.

CAROLYN
What?

GEORGE
The removal of the skull was successful, and the electrodes I've attached keep him cognizant. The fluid he now floats in keeps his brain oxygenated. That being said, it's a delicate device. I wouldn't jostle it.

CAROLYN
You animal!

(He hurls her to the ground)

GEORGE
I'm the animal?! I haven't been rutting with every mangy cur that crosses my path! You wanted to make me a cuckold? This is the recompense.

(CAROLYN weeps)

GEORGE
Dry your eyes, pet. What I've done can be undone.

CAROLYN
You mean...?

GEORGE
Oh yes. Should I choose it, I can return your paramour's cranium to his body. Indeed, if I don't before long, I believe he'll go quite mad.

CAROLYN
I'll do anything, anything you ask. Just tell me what you want of me.

GEORGE
This experiment wasn't for coercion. I have everything I want from you, and you will continue to do as you're told. This was a reminder. You are mine and nothing will ever change that. Do you understand me?

(She nods)

GEORGE
Say it.

CAROLYN
I am yours. Nothing will change that.

GEORGE
That's my girl. *(He closes the cabinet)* I'm keeping Benjamin's body safe. Safe and hidden. If
I think for one moment that you're trying to
uncover it...things will go badly. Am I under-
stood?

CAROLYN
Yes, George.

(He nods. The dog barks outside)

GEORGE
Take a moment with the thing in the jar, then see
to the dog. I'd hate to see him suffer.

*(GEORGE exits. CAROLYN lays her head on the
cabinet and weeps. KAT returns, either in person or
as a voice-over)*

KAT
So Carolyn played the dutiful wife. She cleaned,
she cooked, and she died inside. She wanted more
than anything to help Benjamin, but what could
she do? Even if she found his body, she didn't have
the skills to repair him. And bad as it was for her,
can you even imagine what it was like for him?
Weeks trapped not just in a jar, but in his own
mind. No way to move, or speak, or anything.
Just endless...imprisonment. Wixom was probably
right. Spend too much time like that, you'd probably go completely insane.

*(GEORGE has reentered, attaching something to
the skull)*

GEORGE
Carolyn!

KAT
So there they were, two prisoners with the same warden. And that's just how he wanted it. George Wixom was the kind of man who had to have all the power, all the control. He was the product of older days, and he'd probably die before he ever changed.

(CAROLYN returns. She is more haggard, and a bit dirty)

GEORGE
Christ, woman. You're filthy.

(She mutters something under her breath)

GEORGE
How's that?

CAROLYN
King got away from me.

GEORGE
Oh?

CAROLYN
I had to chase him down a very shabby alley.

GEORGE
Yes, yours is such a life of hardship; married to a doctor, with a fine house and fine clothes.

CAROLYN
I didn't mean to sound ungrateful.

GEORGE
Then you should try harder. Now come. *(He stands away, revealing a phonograph-style device hooked to the skull)* A little something I've been tinkering with. I'm trying to forestall the inevita-

ble mental damage that this particular experiment will cause, with this. *(He taps on the machine)*

CAROLYN
What is it?

GEORGE
My own creation, based on the works of Edison and Bell. If I've calibrated it correctly, it should allow our good friend Benjamin to speak, after a fashion.

CAROLYN
What?!

GEORGE
I think I've been able to successfully access the speech centers of his brain. This device should interpret those signals into recognizable sounds. Hopefully it will lessen the anguish he's most certainly in.

CAROLYN
He...will he be able to hear me?

(GEORGE glares at her)

CAROLYN
Us. Will he be able to hear us?

GEORGE
I think so, but of course, there's only one way to find out. I thought you might want to witness this.

(She nods)

GEORGE
"Thank you, George."

(She stares at him, confused)

GEORGE
You should be thanking me for this kindness, Carolyn.

CAROLYN
(Fighting down her anger) Thank you, George.

GEORGE
That's my girl. *(GEORGE turns on the device, adjust some knobs, etc...)* I haven't actually tried the device yet, so I wouldn't get your hopes up. Even my prodigious intellect has its limits. Let me just...

(Suddenly a horrible scream comes out of the phonograph)

GEORGE
HA!

CAROLYN
Benjamin! Oh god, Benjamin!

GEORGE
My god, I'm a bloody wonder!

CAROLYN
Benjamin, can you hear me?

(The scream just continues)

GEORGE
I know this must be wretched, my dear boy, but you cannot believe the scientific advances you're now part of!

(CAROLYN goes to the jar)

CAROLYN
Can you see me? I'm here! I'm right here!

GEORGE
Of course he can see you. I left the eyes intact. I thought the transition would be easier if he could see his surroundings.

CAROLYN
You have to stop screaming! You have to try and focus!

GEORGE
Oh, let the lad cry out. I imagine he's had that bottled up for a while. *(He laughs at his unintentional joke)* "Bottled up!" Ha!

CAROLYN
There is no devil in hell worse than you.

(Beat)

GEORGE
I beg your pardon?

CAROLYN
To put another person through this kind of torture...whatever human parts are inside you have gone to rot.

(GEORGE strikes her)

GEORGE
This is not torture, wife. This is science. And vengeance. I admit the two fit nicely together.

(BENJAMIN stops screaming)

BENJAMIN
...Carolyn?

CAROLYN
What?

GEORGE
Shhh! *(He goes to the device, adjust it)* Benjamin?
Can you hear us?

BENJAMIN
Carolyn...don't hit...

GEORGE
Try harder, boy. Try to form the words perfectly
in your mind.

BENJAMIN
I...happened...to me...

GEORGE
You're disoriented. That's understandable.

BENJAMIN
...can't feel...anything...

GEORGE
The experiment we were working on...removing
the brain from the body?

BENJAMIN
...what?

GEORGE
I've done it, Ben. And you're the first test subject.

(A blast of static, and BENJAMIN screams again)

GEORGE
Christ, that's getting tiresome.

CAROLYN
Ben, I'm here! Carolyn is here!

GEORGE
Yes. Perhaps he'll listen to his Back-Alley Sally.

(The scream peters off)

CAROLYN
It will be all right, love. You have to listen to me.

BENJAMIN
...Carolyn...?

CAROLYN
Yes. That's it. Say my name.

BENJAMIN
Carolyn.

CAROLYN
Yes.

BENJAMIN
I don't understand what's happened.

GEORGE
Fascinating.

CAROLYN
That's all right. Don't try to think about it. Just relax.

BENJAMIN
I can't. I'm scared.

CAROLYN
(Turning to GEORGE) Please. I'm begging you. Can't you see what you're doing to him?

GEORGE
Of course I can see. I'm going to be goddamn famous.

CAROLYN
(To BENJAMIN) If you can just rest, just sleep. Let your mind wander, like this is all a dream.

When you wake up, everything will be as it was.

BENJAMIN
I'll wake up?

CAROLYN
You will. I promise.

BENJAMIN
And I'll...be me again?

CAROLYN
I'll be here, waiting for you.

GEORGE
Here. Perhaps this will help. *(He puts a cloth over the jar)* I got the idea from the Whaleys next door. They do that with their parakeet.

CAROLYN
Oh god...I'm going to be sick.

GEORGE
Compose yourself. You just cleaned the carpet, after all.

CAROLYN
This is insanity.

GEORGE
I must say, these results are beyond my wildest dreams. I can almost forgive your transgressions because they've yielded...this. *(Turns off the device)* Now if you behave yourself, I'll let you chat with Benjamin from time to time.

CAROLYN
You have to put him back, make him whole again.

GEORGE
Well, yes. Obviously.

(Beat)

CAROLYN
Truly?

GEORGE
My dear, this is only the first part of the experiment. If I'm to prove my genius, I have to show that the brain can safely return to the body.

CAROLYN
You mean it? You'll fix all this?

GEORGE
Of the two of us, Carolyn, I'm the one who keeps my word.

(KAT returns)

KAT
But he didn't. Days went by, a week, two weeks... and Benjamin remained in his jar. The more Carolyn begged, the more George liked seeing her beg. And just like her lover, Carolyn's mind began to shatter. Her happiness lay entirely in the hands of this sadistic bastard. You can only live with that for so long before it breaks you. And George...something was eating at his brain too. Carolyn would come home from running errands and see he'd raided the liquor cabinet. He was going through booze faster than she could restock it. The day finally came where she'd had enough.

(GEORGE collapses in a chair, drunk. He partially undresses, removing his vest, tie & suspenders. CAROLYN returns)

GEORGE
Where have you been?

CAROLYN
I couldn't be in this house a minute longer.

GEORGE
...gone for hours...or days...what day is it?

*(CAROLYN slams a bottle over GEORGE's head.
He collapses. CAROLYN takes a broken piece &
holds it to his throat)*

CAROLYN
This ends today, George. One way or another, this
ends.

GEORGE
...cockchafer...

CAROLYN
You will put Benjamin back together. And you
will do it now.

GEORGE
Or what?

(She presses the glass against him. He cries out)

GEORGE
Kill me and your lover dies, too.

CAROLYN
Then I'll have to take solace in knowing I sent
you to death first.

GEORGE
My little bird has talons. Is that it?

CAROLYN
You did this to me. You broke me and beat me

down until...I have to do this.

(With surprising speed, GEORGE throws her off of him. When she hits the ground, he kicks her)

GEORGE
This ends when I say it ends!

(CAROLYN leaps on him. They struggle. CAROLYN manages to start strangling him with his tie)

CAROLYN
Just...die, you rank bastard!

GEORGE
...stop...please...

CAROLYN
You want me to stop?! Tell me where Benjamin's body is!

GEORGE
...I can't...

CAROLYN
Then sputter and die!

GEORGE
...all right...I will...I...

(She releases him. He collapses to the floor, beaten)

CAROLYN
Take me to his body. Let's get this done.

(He starts to laugh weakly)

CAROLYN
I promise you, this is no joke.

GEORGE
I'm a failure, Carolyn. An utter and complete failure.

CAROLYN
I'm well aware.

GEORGE
I tried. I already tried, but...I failed.

(Beat)

CAROLYN
What did you try?

GEORGE
The nerve endings died so quickly. I hadn't counted on that. A foolish mistake, amateurish. The ganglia, the dorsal root...I couldn't keep it from deteriorating.

CAROLYN
What are you saying?

(GEORGE laughs again)

CAROLYN
What are you saying?!

GEORGE
Benjamin's body died a week ago. Nothing to be done.

(She staggers back)

CAROLYN
No.

GEORGE
I'm afraid so. The only part of him left alive is floating in that jar.

CAROLYN
But you promised...

GEORGE
I truly wanted to see him returned to normal.
Now all my hard work is ruined.

(She grabs GEORGE)

CAROLYN
He was a living being! My love, not some lab rat
for you to dissect!

GEORGE
Shall we agree to disagree?

(She strikes him hard. He collapses again)

CAROLYN
Show me his body.

GEORGE
What?

CAROLYN
You spin lies like spider's silk. Show me his body,
you wretch!

GEORGE
(Laughing again) Oh, I'm afraid that will be rather
difficult.

CAROLYN
Show me!

GEORGE
Well, there's a story to this. *(He stands, but is
unsteady)* Once Benjamin's body passed, it became
clear to me that something had to be done. What
if you brought the police? I couldn't simply leave
his corpse here for anyone to find.

CAROLYN
What have you done?

GEORGE
I'm actually quite proud of this. I couldn't take his body from here. Someone might see me. I couldn't bury him in the basement. Too easy to find. So I…

CAROLYN
What did you do?!

GEORGE
Why not ask King?

(Beat)

CAROLYN
I don't understand.

GEORGE
Benjamin was never a large fellow. It was easy enough to break his body down into…scraps.

CAROLYN
Oh my god…

GEORGE
Yes, dear heart. For the past week, I've been feeding your beloved Benjamin to your beloved dog. There's barely a trace of him left, unless you'd like to inspect King's spoor.

(She staggers into the chair)

GEORGE
Not the end I would've liked for my experiment, but there will be others. Science marches on.

CAROLYN
No…no…

GEORGE

But remember, Carolyn. You brought this on your-self. If you hadn't had such light skirts, Benjamin would be here with us now.

CAROLYN
Oh god...

GEORGE
But what am I saying? Benjamin is here with us!

(He goes to the cabinet, opens it. He begins to turn on the speaking device)

GEORGE
Come along, pet! I'm sure the horrible news will be easier on Benjamin were it to come from you.

(She rises, slowly going to a shelf on the wall)

GEORGE
Give us a moment, Benny boy! Carolyn has a dog food recipe she'd like to share with you!

(He laughs, his back to her. She grabs a candlestick)

GEORGE
Nobody takes care of a dog like Carolyn. And I do mean No Body!

(He laughs again. She comes up behind him and clubs him with the candlestick. He drops)

GEORGE
...good Christ...

(Expressionless, she proceeds to club him repeat-edly until he is clearly dead. She collapses on the ground. After a bit--)

BENJAMIN
...Carolyn?

(She sits up, looks at the jar)

BENJAMIN
I can't see anything anymore.

(She almost removes the cloth from the jar, but stops)

BENJAMIN
Have I been sleeping?

CAROLYN
Yes, my love.

BENJAMIN
I want to wake up. Can I please wake up now?

CAROLYN
Soon. Soon.

BENJAMIN
I'm very scared.

CAROLYN
I know.

BENJAMIN
And I miss you. I miss you so much.

(She begins to weep)

BENJAMIN
I don't understand what's happened.

CAROLYN
That's all right.

BENJAMIN
I can hear you, but I can't see you.

(She tentatively removes the cloth)

BENJAMIN
Carolyn.

CAROLYN
Hello, Ben.

BENJAMIN
I can see you.

CAROLYN
I can see you, too.

BENJAMIN
Beautiful. So beautiful.

(She places her hand on the jar)

BENJAMIN
Why can't I feel you?

CAROLYN
It's...hard to explain.

BENJAMIN
I'm scared. I'm so scared.

CAROLYN
Shh. It's all right.

BENJAMIN
I want to hold you.

CAROLYN
I know.

BENJAMIN
I can't feel anything. Anything at all.

CAROLYN
Don't worry, darling. You don't have to be scared
anymore.

BENJAMIN
I just want to be with you.

CAROLYN
I know.

BENJAMIN
That's all I've ever wanted.

CAROLYN
We'll be together soon. Soon, and forever. *(She kisses the jar)* Just know...just know how much I love you.

BENJAMIN
Carolyn?

(She pushes the jar to the ground. It shatters, and the skull lies there, disconnected from the machine. A broken voice fades out of the phonograph)

BENJAMIN
...carolyn...carolyn...carolyn...

(She screams in anguish as the lights return to the campfire. KAT is there. MAYA soon rejoins her)

KAT
My dad told me that story when I was fifteen. It was...late September, early October. Somewhere in there. Jim Warshowski had asked me to the homecoming dance. My first dance ever. I was so excited and I come down the stairs and my dad's got the camera ready. I was in this just awful red dress, and he tells me to sit down. All I can think is "going to a dance going to a dance going to a dance". So I sit down, and he throws a couple logs on the fire and launches into the story of George Wixom. He finishes right before Jim shows up,

corsage in hand. We went out and danced and drank and fooled around...and the whole time, that fucking story was in my head. The whole fucking time.

MAYA
I'm sorry.

KAT
That was my dad all the way. Half the time, he's telling me how important it is to not be alone, you know? "Find a nice fella, settle down, have 8 kids," whatever. Then he hits me with stories like that. This is why I have a dim view on marriage.

MAYA
It's not always like that though.

KAT
Sure. I get that. But most the people I know who've gotten married? Miserable. They rush into this thing 'cause they're terrified of being alone, and then year after year they carve away another part of themselves for the sake of their partner, until they're basically unrecognizable. It's messed up.

MAYA
You have spent a lot of time thinking about this.

KAT
I really, really have.

MAYA
So...are you trying to scare me away? From marrying Johnny, I mean.

KAT
Whoa. Are you guys talking about that already?

MAYA
I mean…in the vaguest terms, maybe.

(Beat. KAT thinks on it)

KAT
Honestly, I'm the last person to tell anyone how to live their life. Most of my work with the DNR is about doing shit by myself, because that's how I like it. But you love Johnny, yeah?

MAYA
I do. I really do.

KAT
Could you see your life with him? Being part of this family?

MAYA
Actually, yeah.

(KAT smiles at her)

KAT
I feel like you're kinda damaged.

MAYA
OK.

KAT
But our kind of damaged.

MAYA
Is that a good thing?

KAT
I think so. Others might think different, but to hell with them.

MAYA
(Raising her beer) To hell with them!

(They clink beers and drink. JOHNNY & MARCUS return with hot dogs. JOHNNY embraces MAYA)

JOHNNY
I come bearing wieners!

MAYA
Oh my god.

KAT
Class act, Johnny. Class act.

JOHNNY
It's a funny word! Weiners! Weinersweinersweiners weinersweinersweiners....

MARCUS
I thought I had marshmallows for s'mores, but a damn mouse got to 'em.

KAT
You know that mouse traps exist, right?

MARCUS
Hush up, you.

JOHNNY
You two have some good old-fashioned girl talk?

MAYA
I...yeah. Yeah, I'd say so.

KAT
For sure.

MARCUS
Which one did you tell her?

(KAT just stares at him)

MARCUS
We were gone long enough. I figured you told her

one of our stories.

KAT
George Wixom's Wife.

JOHNNY
Oh for crap's sake! You told my girlfriend George Wixom's Wife?

KAT
Just kinda came up.

(JOHNNY goes to MAYA)

JOHNNY
Baby, I'll never remove your skull and put it in a jar.

MAYA
This is why I love you.

JOHNNY
That and my weiner?

KAT
Come on!

MARCUS
...really should've looked harder for s'mores.

KAT
I'm gonna go find some sticks.

JOHNNY
Sticks for the wieners?

KAT
There are no words for how much I hate you.

JOHNNY
Impossible. I'm unhatable.

MAYA
He is kinda unhatable.

JOHNNY
See?

KAT
Young and naïve. She's young and naïve. *(Walks off)*

MARCUS
That's something.

JOHNNY
Right? Unbelievable.

MAYA
I'm sorry, what?

MARCUS
I have never seen Kat warm up to someone so fast.

MAYA
Is that what that was?

JOHNNY
Absolutely. I'm not gonna lie, I was sweating bullets about you two meeting.

MAYA
She's awesome!

MARCUS
The words most often used for Katrina are "acquired taste."

JOHNNY
My first girlfriend? I left her with Kat for ten minutes, I came back, and she was sobbing.

MAYA
Come on.

MARCUS
He's tellin' the truth. Jenny Newsome, right?

JOHNNY
Oh Jenny. Sweet, simple Jenny.

MARCUS
What happened to her anyway?

(*JOHNNY just shakes his head*)

MARCUS
Oh shit. Right.

MAYA
What?

JOHNNY
It's...don't worry about it.

MAYA
Something bad?

JOHNNY
No, not like...it's a long story.

MARCUS
Johnny's had some bad break-ups. Like, the kind that Vikings used to write epic poems about.

MAYA
Wow.

JOHNNY
Part of why I took so long asking you out. I just... sometimes I don't feel like I'm dating someone. It feels more like I'm inflicting myself on them.

MAYA
Oh. I like that.

JOHNNY
You do?

MAYA
I mean, the way you said that. I like that.

MARCUS
Boy's got a way with words.

MAYA
I know. The others in our program hate him.

MARCUS
Is that right?

MAYA
Oh yeah. He seems like this big goof...

JOHNNY
Fair.

MAYA
...and then he turns this stuff in for peer edit-
ing and it's just...it's amazing. Lyrical, but really
simple. He gets this really intense emotion through
in a way that sort of sneaks up on you.

(MARCUS puts his hand on JOHNNY's shoulder)

MARCUS
He gets that from his old man.

MAYA
I wondered.

MARCUS
Oh yeah. Mitch was this big fella, larger than life.
Flannels and overalls and dirty boots. But when

he sat down to tell a story...

JOHNNY
It was like all the lights dimmed, just because he was talking.

MARCUS
Exactly. Now I'm no slouch, but I never met a man who could weave a tale like my brother. It was like you said about Johnny. Stuff would just sneak up on you. The funny parts, the scary parts, the things that made you wanna weep...it was all there the whole time, but he'd tell it in a way where you didn't notice it til the end.

MAYA
I wish I could've met him.

MARCUS
Oh, he'd have liked you. That's for sure.

MAYA
Really?

JOHNNY
Dad had an eye for the pretty girls.

MAYA
Shut up.

MARCUS
You got a sweet spirit. He liked that. Mitch could be a grade-A son of a bitch if he thought you'd done wrong by someone he loved. But the truth is, he'd just get worked up 'cause his damn heart was so big.

JOHNNY
Nothing mattered to him like family. No one Kat

ever dated was good enough. And she was kind of a...know what? I'm gonna stop there.

MARCUS
Hell, like you were any better. Johnny's got a long history of picking them dumb and pretty. You're a pleasant change.

MAYA
Because I'm not pretty?

MARCUS
Wait. I didn't mean...

MAYA
It's ok. I'm just busting your chops.

MARCUS
(Laughing) Oh, I like her. I like her a lot. So which one did you like better? The Scalped Man or George Wixom's Wife?

MAYA
Oh. Um...I don't know. They're both really different.

MARCUS
It's ok. Kat's out there. You won't hurt her feelings.

MAYA
I liked them both, but...

JOHNNY
There's one thing Maya likes more than scary stories.

MARCUS
Don't say "wieners." I'm begging you.

JOHNNY
She likes love stories best.

MARCUS
Oh. Gotcha.

MAYA
I can't help it. My folks are these big romantics
and...

MARCUS
Girl, never apologize for loving love. Best thing in
the world. But you know you liked my story best.

(MAYA laughs)

MARCUS
Come on now. It's all about love! Brotherly love.

MAYA
And ghosts. And bloody scalps.

MARCUS
Just like Breakfast at Tiffany's.

JOHNNY
At least Kat's story has some romance to it.

MARCUS
Like hell.

JOHNNY
She lost everything because she loved a head in
a jar!

MARCUS
That's not love! That's...some sort of weird, sick
devotion.

JOHNNY
Yes. Called love.

MAYA
None of them are things you're gonna see in a Valentine card.

MARCUS
Hallmark is full of cowards is why.

JOHNNY
So you're saying you want a love story?

MAYA
I wouldn't say no.

MARCUS
All right, but that's not what tonight's about. I'm sorry, I don't mean to piss on your boots, but...

MAYA
You're telling scary stories to honor Johnny's father. I get it.

JOHNNY
Right, but there's nothing saying we can't do both.

(Beat)

MARCUS
Which story you thinkin' about, son?

JOHNNY
You know which one.

MARCUS
You sure?

JOHNNY
I am. 100% sure.

MAYA
Ooo! Why all the mysterious?

MARCUS
Well now...the story Johnny's talking about...
it's one we don't usually tell. Pretty much never,
really.

JOHNNY
But it was Dad's favorite. You know it was.

MARCUS
It was that.

MAYA
Why don't you tell it?

MARCUS
Because it really happened.

(Beat)

MAYA
I really wanna hear this story.

(JOHNNY looks at MARCUS)

MARCUS
Your call, Johnny. I trust you.

JOHNNY
Cool.

*(He takes MAYA's hand. The lights change, and
the scene changes behind them to a living room in
a 1970s farmhouse)*

JOHNNY
So this story...it's like Uncle Marcus said. Not a
lot of people know about it, but it's all true.

MAYA
Ok.

JOHNNY
It happened on Halloween...

MAYA
Of course.

JOHNNY
October 31st, 1976. It actually happened not far
from here.

MAYA
Ooo!

JOHNNY
It was in an old farmhouse, but the man who
lived there wasn't a farmer. He was a Professor
over at Ferris State; one of those guys who liked
the big houses, the history, but had no interest in
the land. His name was...shit. Uncle Marcus, what
was his name?

MARUS
Carl. Carl Welliver.

JOHNNY
Right. Professor Welliver. Smart man, funny,
charming...maybe too charming. Too charming
for a single man with a lot of female students,
know what I mean?

MAYA
I don't like him already.

JOHNNY
So the story goes, he's having a...private Halloween
party in 1976.

*(MARCUS becomes CARL, MAYA becomes
JENNY. The living room is warm, with a few*

Halloween decorations. JENNY is alone in the room, listening to the radio. Swamp Witch by Jim Stafford is playing, & she sways to the music. CARL soon enters with a bottle of wine and two glasses)

JENNY
I love this song.

CARL
I can tell.

JENNY
So creepy and Halloween-y. *(She stops dancing, looks at him)*

CARL
Don't stop on my account.

JENNY
Should we really be having wine?

CARL
Spiced wine, actually.

JENNY
I mean, what will people think?

CARL
I don't see anyone here. Just you and me.

(She walks to him)

CARL
And I won't tell if you don't.

(He kisses her. She laughs)

JENNY
You know what they say about you, Dr. Welliver?

CARL
What do they say about me, Jenny?

JENNY
That you're a bad man.

CARL
Is that right?

JENNY
I mean, I just wanted to talk about my Abnormal Psych paper.

CARL
Is that right?

JENNY
These aren't your regular office hours. And this isn't your office.

CARL
I have an office upstairs. Does that help?

JENNY
It doesn't hurt.

(He turns off the radio)

JENNY
Aw! They were playing Spooky Songs of Halloween. I wanted to hear *Don't Fear The Reaper.*

CARL
You said you wanted to talk about your paper. Let's talk.

(He sits on the couch & pours the wine. She joins him)

CARL
So you decided to focus on the psychology behind

modern cults. Marshall Applewhite's group... um...

JENNY
Human Individual Metamorphosis.

CARL
That's right. Here.

(He gives her the glass. They drink as they speak)

CARL
Really interesting stuff. I'm particularly fascinated by the way they incorporate modern science fiction with archaic religious philosophy.

JENNY
Their ties to the Book of Revelations are really bizarre.

CARL
Don't judge their actions, Jenny. Observe from a place of emotional distance.

JENNY
Yes sir, Dr. Welliver sir.

CARL
What specifically did you want to discuss with me?

JENNY
Well, they have a belief system that's constantly in flux, I think.

CARL
For example?

JENNY
Well, they follow the Ancient Astronaut hypothesis, but their leader also thinks the aliens are communicating with him through

episodes of *Star Trek*.

CARL
And you think that doesn't hold true?

JENNY
I think it's interesting that aliens who supposedly visited Earth millions of years ago have decided that an American television show is the best way to reach out. Wouldn't an extraterrestrial intelligence be better served with some sort of real mass communication?

CARL
You're trying to rationalize it through your perspective, not Applewhite's.

JENNY
Fair enough.

CARL
You also pointed out some of the cult's behaviors that I found worth noting.

JENNY
Such as?

CARL
The need to prepare themselves for ascension. The communal living, the surrendering of personal property...

JENNY
Giving up sex completely.

CARL
That one caught my attention, yes.

JENNY
Can you imagine? The only way to experience

the true nature of Heaven is to abandon inter-course?

CARL
Shocking.

JENNY
No offence to Marshall Applewhite, but I do not want to get into Heaven that way.

CARL
Who would?

JENNY
Not me.

CARL
Not me either.

(They've moved closer)

JENNY
So what do you really think of my work, Dr. Welliver?

CARL
I think that the practices of the Human Individual Metamorphosis only work on paper.

(They kiss. It grows more passionate. Suddenly, there is a knock at the door)

JENNY
Were...were you expecting someone?

CARL
No.

(Knocking. Someone calls "trick-r-treat" from outside)

JENNY
Do you usually get trick-r-treaters this far from the city?

CARL
One or two a year, maybe.

JENNY
They're really dedicated.

(The knocking continues. CARL calls off)

CARL
All right! Give me a damn minute! *(Looks to JENNY)* Class is not dismissed.

(He rummages around for something to give the trick-r-treaters. He finds some gum)

CARL
They're going to get chewing gum, and they're going to like it.

(He opens the door. Two 20-somethings are there. They wear strange, terrifying masks, but the rest of their clothes are typical 70s attire)

CARL
Um...hello?

(They wave, then hold out their bags)

CARL
Aren't you a little old for trick-or-treating?

(They shake their bags)

CARL
Here.

(He drops the gum in their bags. They look inside

as he slams the door)

JENNY
What was that?

CARL
I'm not sure. Students who probably need to sleep
it off would be my guess.

JENNY
Kids these days, right?

CARL
You're not calling me old, are you?

JENNY
I would never.

CARL
I just turned fifty.

JENNY
Mm-hmm.

CARL
I still have a lot of life in me.

JENNY
Is this another lecture, Professor? Or are you
going to show me?

*(They return to fooling around. Knocking on the
door again)*

CARL
For christ's sake... *(Shouts over his shoulder)* Go
home already!

(The knocking becomes pounding)

CARL
What the hell is this?

(He goes to the door and throws it open. No one is there)

CARL
Fucking kids....

(He suddenly notices a crow nailed to the front of the door)

CARL
Jesus! *(He slams the door)*

JENNY
Carl?

CARL
Those kids...they...oh my god..

JENNY
What is it?

CARL
Call the police. Now.

JENNY
What?

CARL
Call the police! NOW!

(She scrambles for the phone. He goes to a drawer, removes a gun)

JENNY
You have a gun?

CARL
Are you calling?!

JENNY
Give me a second!

(She is about to dial, then stops. She stares at CARL)

CARL
What is it?

(She just holds the phone up. Laughter can be heard through it)

CARL
What the hell is this?

(Knocking on the door, loud and frantic)

JENNY
Oh my god. Tell them to go away!

(He makes sure the gun is loaded, then heads to the door. He's about to open it when suddenly the knocking moves to the windows. We can see the masked faces there. JENNY screams. The knocking returns to the door. CARL runs to it and a loud crash is heard offstage)

JENNY
No no no no...

CARL
I have a gun, you little punks!

JENNY
What's back there?

CARL
The back door. Shit!

(He runs to it. As soon as he's gone, JENNY realizes he didn't lock the front door. She runs to it, but it swings open as she gets there. The masked people enter)

JENNY
Carl!

(The GIRL grabs JENNY)

GIRL
You're not my mommy!

(She spins her around as CARL returns. She puts a knife to JENNY's throat. CARL stops)

CARL
Look, you don't have to do this.

BOY
Gum? Really? That's bogue, man.

CARL
What?

BOY
I wanted like a Marathon bar! Or a Three Musketeers!

GIRL
SPACE DUST!

BOY
Dude, you ever have Space Dust? It's killer. You toss 'em in your mouth and they kind of explode or something. I'm not describing it right.

CARL
What do you want?

BOY
Did I not just tell you? I want a Marathon bar!

GIRL
SPACE DUST!

BOY
My girl wants Space Dust.

CARL
I don't have any of those things.

BOY
Really?

CARL
Really.

BOY
Ok, let's go. *(He starts to leave, then laughs)* Yeah, you're not getting off that easy.

(He pokes JENNY with a knife, drawing blood. She cries out)

BOY
Or was he? Huh?

CARL
Don't! Don't hurt her.

BOY
You care about this little bunny, yeah?

CARL
You don't have to hurt anyone.

BOY
Of course I don't. But I'm gonna.

CARL
Let her go, and I'll put down the gun.

BOY
You don't tell us what to do. This is our house.

(The GIRL tosses JENNY to the BOY, who holds her, knife to her throat)

GIRL
Daddy?

CARL
What?

(She hugs CARL)

BOY
Careful, baby! He's got a gun!

GIRL
Daddy daddy daddy daddy!

CARL
Let go of me!

(He pushes her to the ground. She starts to sob)

BOY
Aw man! Look what you did!

(CARL points the gun at her)

CARL
Let Jenny go.

BOY
No.

CARL
I'll shoot your girlfriend.

BOY
I don't think you will.

CARL
I will. I swear to Christ I will.

BOY
No, you won't. You don't care about her. You don't care about anyone.

(CARL draws back the hammer on the gun. BOY lets JENNY go)

BOY
There.

(JENNY runs to CARL. GIRL leaps at them in a rage. CARL fires. GIRL drops to the ground)

BOY
Holy shit. You did it.

(CARL points the gun at BOY)

BOY
Whoa. Maintain.

CARL
Jenny, call the police.

(JENNY goes for the phone, but stumbles)

BOY
Whoops.

CARL
Jenny?

JENNY
I don't...I feel weird...

(She suddenly begins to convulse. It is quick and violent, and she drops onto the couch. CARL goes to her, his gun still on the BOY)

BOY
Yeah, I put a little somethin' on the knife, just in case.

(Suddenly, the GIRL stands up and grabs CARL's gun and breaks his arm. He cries out)

GIRL
I'm sorry, daddy.

CARL
Oh god...what the hell...?

BOY
She's tougher than she looks. Just like our mom.

(The BOY joins them, cradling the dying JENNY in his lap)

BOY
Here's the thing, Professor. Me and my girl...we got a family coming, so we need a place to settle down. A nice place, middle of nowhere. A place where we can blend in.

GIRL
Baby?

BOY
Yeah?

GIRL
She's looking a little...green.

(The BOY looks at JENNY. As he speaks, he finds his knife)

BOY
We're not bad people. Not like you. We just want a place to live off the land with our kid. Or kids. We haven't decided yet.

GIRL
I want at least two. Three would be...

BOY
Babe, one thing at a time.

GIRL
Sorry.

(He slits JENNY's throat. CARL tries to cry out, but GIRL holds his mouth. BOY speaks casually as he kills JENNY)

BOY
It took us a while to find you, Dr. Welliver. We didn't have a lot to go on. Mom didn't like talking about you, about the things you did to her. Sounds like you've been messing around with students for a long time.

GIRL
A drunk "no" is still a "no," daddy.

BOY
So yeah, you're gonna die. Home invasion type of thing. Turns out there are some sick, scary people out there. And they look just like everyone else. *(Removes his mask)* And when you're gone, this place is gonna go to your only living relative. A blood test will prove that out.

GIRL
Thank you, daddy. Thank you thank you thank you.

BOY
You want me to do it?

GIRL
No. He's my dad, not yours. Mama said this is how it's done.

BOY
I'm right here beside you, babe.

GIRL
I know.

*(He gives the GIRL the knife, and she stabs CARL
repeatedly. They push the two bodies to the ground,
and hold each other on the couch)*

BOY
You ok?

GIRL
Mm-hmm.

BOY
We can talk about it if you want to.

GIRL
It's fine. Really. I didn't actually know him. And
look at this place. It's perfect.

BOY
You're perfect.

GIRL
No, you're perfect!

*(They kiss. She winces as he touches her bullet
wound)*

BOY
Oh! I'm sorry.

GIRL
It's ok. It's already healing up.

BOY
Cool.

GIRL
Sorry I went a little nuts before. Seeing him there,
with her...I don't know.

BOY
Babe, you don't have to apologize for anything.
(He pulls some candy out of their Halloween bags)
Happy Halloween and I love you.

GIRL
Happy Halloween and I love you.

(She eats the candy without removing her mask. Lights return to the campfire. During the transition, everyone returns to their previous roles)

JOHNNY
See? Romantic. *(He reads MAYA's expression)* OK, maybe not conventionally romantic, but...

MAYA
I loved it.

JOHNNY
You loved it?

MAYA
I mean, it's sick and it's twisted, but...yeah. It was great.

(JOHNNY looks to MARCUS, who smiles approvingly. JOHNNY hugs her as KAT returns with some sticks)

KAT
What'd I miss?

MARCUS
Johnny told her the story.

KAT
Which one?

MARCUS
Take a guess.

(KAT looks at the two of them)

KAT
Holy shit. Really?

JOHNNY
Really.

KAT
Johnny, you...really?

JOHNNY
I did. I really did.

MAYA
I loved it!

KAT
I'll be damned.

MAYA
So wait...that whole story. It actually happened?

JOHNNY
Absolutely.

MAYA
When did they catch those two...the killers?

KAT
They didn't.

MAYA
Oh. Um...I don't understand.

JOHNNY
What do you mean?

MAYA
If they never caught them, then how do you know what actually happened to Dr. Welliver?

(KAT sits with them)

MARCUS
The boy in that story...that was my brother.
Mitchell.

KAT
And the girl...

MAYA
His sister.

JOHNNY
Half-sister, actually.

KAT
...was our mom.

MAYA
What?

JOHNNY
It's the truth. I know it sounds messed up, but it's
the truth. Hand to god.

MARCUS
See, they had the same mom. Well, we all did.
Carlotta Carver. And she...

(MAYA starts to laugh)

MAYA
Holy shit! That was awesome! I totally believed
you!

JOHNNY
We're not joking.

MAYA
Really? So your parents were these, like, incestual
1970s murderers who...*(She reads their expres-*

sions and falls silent)

KAT
They were a lot more than that.

MAYA
What is this? What are you talking about?

MARCUS
Maya, that story Johnny told you...it's a story we almost never tell. It means something.

JOHNNY
It means that I love you. I love you more than anything, and I want you to be a part of my family. *(Gets down on one knee)*

MAYA
Oh my god...

JOHNNY
But the thing is...Maya, being a Carver...there's a lot you need to know about us. I brought you here because I trust you. And I had to make sure Kat and Marcus would trust you too.

KAT
I do. I trust her.

MARCUS
You picked a winner, kid.

JOHNNY
You'll meet the rest of the family eventually, but it was important that...

MAYA
Wait. I thought you were the last three.

(JOHNNY looks to his family)

MAYA
You told me there were only three Carvers left.

JOHNNY
That's...not entirely accurate.

MAYA
What do you mean?

MARCUS
Our kin...the other Carvers...are all over this country. It's true, there aren't as many of us left as there once was.

KAT
But we're the only ones left who can pass.

MAYA
Pass? Pass for what?

JOHNNY
Human.

(Beat. MAYA backs away)

MAYA
You can't be serious.

JOHNNY
It's true, Maya. Our family has been here for a very, very long time, doing the work we were born to do.

MAYA
I...I still feel like you're screwing with me.

MARCUS
It's a hard thing to understand, but he's not lying. We walk with the rest of the world, but we're apart from it too. We watch, we listen, and we tell our stories.

MAYA
Why?

KAT
Because there's a flaw in the human design. You
all think you're supposed to know everything.
You keep searching and exploring and poking
your nose where it doesn't belong.

JOHNNY
Our family exists because you're not supposed
to know everything. There are things out there,
things in the dark, that are supposed to stay in
the dark.

MARCUS
For a real long time…hell, since before our ances-
tor rode through Sleepy Hollow…we've been
telling our cautionary tales. We're here to keep
you afraid of the night. Afraid of closets and base-
ments and the strange places in the woods.

KAT
That's where the rest of our family lives.

JOHNNY
We're here to keep you safe. There's a reason you
shouldn't go to those places. The stories we tell…
they've saved so many lives. Or they used to.

MARCUS
That's why there aren't as many of us left. The
more people learn, the more they see, the harder
it is for us to stay hidden.

KAT
You stop believing in our stories. And when that
happens, people go to those places, and they don't
come back.

JOHNNY
I know how nuts this sounds, baby. I do. But it's all true. Every single word of it.

KAT
The woman who saw the soldier's ghost, the skull in the jar...they're part of our family.

JOHNNY
What I'm asking you...Maya, will you be part of this family too? *(He goes to her)*

MAYA
All those stories I've heard, ever since I was a kid...the ghost stories and legends about things with fangs and claws and...you started them.

JOHNNY
Yes.

MAYA
And they weren't just to scare kids around a camp-fire. You were telling us what's out there, waiting for us if we get too close.

JOHNNY
Yes.

MAYA
Are...are you aliens?

(The Carvers laugh)

JOHNNY
Babe, no. There's no such thing as aliens.

KAT
We've been here as long as humans have. We're the fanged, clawed things that lived in caves.

MARCUS
And there's always a few, like us, that look like
everyone else. Well, most of the time. Sometimes
we marry our kin, but that's the old way. Mitchell
was one of the last to do that. Because…well,
we're not like everyone else.

MAYA
You're monsters.

JOHNNY
Yeah.

MAYA
And you're asking me to be a part of that? A part
of the things hiding under the bed?

JOHNNY
I am.

(Beat)

MAYA
Hell yes.

*(She kisses him. MARCUS & KAT go to her. They
embrace)*

MARCUS
Jesus Christ, it'll be good to have some new blood
in the family!

MAYA
This is incredible! I can't even…Holy shit!

KAT
You won't get credit for it, but you're going to
help make the stories that go on forever.

MAYA
I gotta sit down. This is…I gotta sit down.

(She sits. JOHNNY joins her)

JOHNNY
Maya, I've loved you for so long, but I was an idiot. I thought I had all the time in the world, you know? But when Dad died...I knew it was time to get my life right, and I knew it had to be you.

MAYA
Really?

JOHNNY
You don't always go after the ones you really want. You go after the ones you know you can get.

KAT
What he's saying is that he's a chicken-shit and you were so great, you scared him half to death.

MAYA
You? The guy who's related to every terrifying thing I've ever heard about, and you were scared of me?

JOHNNY
I'm a complicated guy.

MARCUS
I need to get some champagne or something. What the hell am I thinking?

MAYA
Wait. Johnny, do we have to move back here? Or...

JOHNNY
No no no. We can live wherever we want.

MARCUS
For the record, I wouldn't hate it if you moved

back here.

KAT
Marcus! They just got engaged! Give them some breathing room.

MARCUS
Right. Yep. Let me just...champagne. *(He hurries off)*

MAYA
Oh my god...I have so many questions.

JOHNNY
Ask me anything.

MAYA
So what you were saying...you're not actually human?

JOHNNY
Nope. We're close, but nope. That's why mom didn't die when she got shot.

MAYA
That's insane.

KAT
Oh honey, there's so much more insane coming your way.

MAYA
Did...did I just agree to marry into The Munsters?

KAT
God, I love that show.

JOHNNY
No. No no no. 90% of the time, we're gonna be just like any other couple.

MAYA
But the other 10%?

KAT
That's the fun 10%.

MAYA
Oh my god. You're going to be my sister.

KAT
I...yeah, I guess so.

(MAYA hugs her, taking her by surprise)

MAYA
I've never had a sister! Or a brother! Or...oh my god!

KAT
You really are a hugger.

MAYA
I really am.

KAT
This is gonna take some getting used to.

MAYA
My family is so tiny. This is gonna be great!

JOHNNY
Speaking of that, we should talk about, you know, the kids thing.

(Beat)

MAYA
What?

JOHNNY
Know what? I'm dumb. We don't have to talk about that now.

MAYA
Johnny…

JOHNNY
We're young. We're super young still. Young and sexy. We can still do tons of stuff before we have a baby.

KAT
OK, see? That's our dad talking. He kept getting so freaked out because there were so few Carvers left. "You and your brother gotta start having babies."

JOHNNY
Our dad just really wanted to know the line would continue before he died. He never got to see a grandkid, but that doesn't matter. All that matters is that the line will continue.

KAT
It has to.

MAYA
Johnny.

JOHNNY
Am I talking too much? I know I…*(He reads her expression)* Babe? What is it?

MAYA
Can we…can we talk alone?

KAT
What's wrong, sweetie?

MAYA
I don't…Johnny, we need to talk about this later, ok.

JOHNNY
I'm sorry if I said something that freaked you out.
I figured once you got past the whole "who we
really are thing," that...

KAT
You can't have children, can you?

(Long beat. JOHNNY stares at MAYA. She tears
up a little)

JOHNNY
What?

KAT
You said you were sick when you were little. This
is because of that, isn't it?

(MAYA nods)

JOHNNY
But...but it's...I mean, it's not like there's no way,
right? I mean, there's fertility clinics! There's
specialists who ...there are options!

MAYA
Not for me.

(JOHNNY backs away, trying & failing to reign
in his emotions)

JOHNNY
...no no no...

MAYA
I'm sorry. I wanted to tell you for so long, but I
never knew how. How do you say that to the man
you love?

JOHNNY
Jesus Christ! (He grabs her roughly) You should've

told me! Don't you know what this…Fuck!

MAYA
Johnny! Please!

(He lets her go, pacing manically)

MAYA
Just listen to me! Kat, please just tell him to…

KAT
Oh, honey. I wish I could. But what you've done to him….

MAYA
What I…?

KAT
…there's no coming back from that.

MAYA
Johnny, we love each other! This is one thing, one little thing! We can get past this!

JOHNNY
No!

MAYA
If you really want a kid, maybe we could adopt or…

JOHNNY
Don't you get it?! It wouldn't be my child! It wouldn't be a Carver!

MAYA
That doesn't matter!

JOHNNY
It's the only thing that matters!

(MAYA falls silent, backs away)

JOHNNY
Maya, there are so few of us left. Those of us who
can breed, have to.

MAYA
But Kat! She hasn't...

JOHNNY
She still has time.

KAT
(Taking JOHNNY's hand) I'm sorry. I'm so so
sorry.

MAYA
You can't do this. You can't end what we have
because of this.

JOHNNY
I love you.

MAYA
I know. I love you too.

JOHNNY
If I'd known, if you told me...I can't take it back,
Maya. The story of my family...you know it now.

MAYA
I know.

JOHNNY
You don't, though. You really don't.

(MARCUS returns with the champagne)

MARCUS
What's going on?

JOHNNY
Marcus...oh Jesus, I can't...

MARCUS
What is it, son?

KAT
It's bad.

MAYA
Johnny?

KAT
She can't have children.

MARCUS
Oh no. Oh god no. *(He looks to MAYA)* Maya girl, you gotta be straight with me, right here, right now. Is this a "difficult to have children," or a "cannot under any circumstances have children?"

(She says nothing)

MARCUS
Answer me!

MAYA
There's no way.

MARCUS
Goddammit! *(He grabs her roughly)*

MAYA
Hey!

MARCUS
You know what you gotta do, Johnny.

JOHNNY
No!

MARCUS
This isn't an option! It's gotta be done, and you gotta do it.

JOHNNY
I can't.

MAYA
Let me go!

(MARCUS covers her mouth, turns her to face JOHNNY)

KAT
He's right. This is the way we've always done it. He knows better than anyone.

MARCUS
It damn near killed me to do it to my Clara, but I did it because I'm a Carver.

JOHNNY
Then fuck it. I don't want to be a Carver.

MARCUS
You don't have a say in that.

(JOHNNY looks to KAT)

JOHNNY
Please. Please, I can't do this.

(KAT goes to him, puts her hands on his shoulders)

KAT
You can. You have to.

JOHNNY
She doesn't deserve this.

KAT
You're right. She doesn't. But that's not what this

is about.

(Beat)

JOHNNY
I know.

(KAT squeezes his hand)

KAT
I'm here. I'm right here.

(JOHNNY lets go of her hand and walks to MAYA. He touches her face)

JOHNNY
I'm so sorry.

(He lifts her chin and tears into her throat with his bare teeth. It is very violent and bloody, but over quickly. MARCUS lets her drop as JOHNNY stands there covered in blood. After a moment of shock, he begins to weep. MARCUS and KAT go to him)

MARCUS
Oh, son. You just let it out.

(KAT embraces him)

KAT
It's ok, Johnny. It's ok.

(He gently removes himself from the embrace)

MARCUS
This was a hard thing you did, but you did it like a Carver. Your daddy would've been real proud.

JOHNNY
My dad was a sick freak.

(JOHNNY starts to walk off. KAT goes to him, but he motions for her to stay put)

JOHNNY
Leave me alone, Kat. Just...I want to be alone.

KAT
OK. We'll be here when you come back.

JOHNNY
I know.

(JOHNNY exits. MARCUS sits, emotionally drained. KAT sits with him)

KAT
How you holding up, old man?

MARCUS
I've done what that poor boy had to do. Saw a cousin of mine do it in '69 too. It never gets easier.

KAT
No, but it had to be done.

MARCUS
Yep.
KAT
I'm worried about him.

MARCUS
You're always worried about him.

KAT
I know.

MARCUS
He's hurting right now, a kind of hurt I hope to God you never experience. But he'll come out the other side of it.

KAT
How do you know?

MARCUS
I did. *(Puts his arm around her)* We live a hard life, and it's made harder 'cause we can't really share it. In the end, all a Carver has is his family.

KAT
I liked her, Uncle Marcus.

MARCUS
So did I, darln'. She was as good as they come.

KAT
I don't want to do it.

MARCUS
We have to.

KAT
What if Johnny…?

MARCUS
It'll be harder on him to see her like he left her. Besides, we can't just leave her here for someone to find.

(KAT rubs her face in her hands)

KAT
Oh fuck me…

MARCUS
I'll walk you through it. You're not doing this alone.

KAT
Thanks.

MARCUS
Sure. *(He takes out his knife and begins to cut pieces off of MAYA's flesh)*

KAT
Marcus?

MARCUS
Yeah?

KAT
I don't want to go through this.

MARCUS
"This" meaning…?

KAT
The falling in love thing. The settling down thing. What's the point if it ends up like this?

MARCUS
It doesn't, usually. And you know what? Love don't care what you want. It finds you all the same.

KAT
You sound like a Billy Joel song.

(MARCUS chuckles)

MARCUS
You'll find someone. And you'll get married and
have a whole herd of little ones.

KAT
How do you know?

MARCUS
Because you're your father's daughter.

*(He stands. He's placed pieces of MAYA's flesh on
the sticks KAT brought in earlier)*

MARCUS
Here. *(Hands her one)* For what it's worth, Maya,
we're sorry as hell. We'd have been lucky to call
you kin.

(They put the meat over the fire)

KAT
Know what?

MARCUS
What?

KAT
At the very least, this will make one hell of a
story.

*(They watch as the meat cooks on the fire. Lights
fade)*

END OF PLAY

ABOUT THE PLAYWRIGHT

Joseph Zettelmaier is a Michigan-based playwright and four-time nominee for the Steinberg/American Theatre Critics Association Award for best new play, first in 2006 for ALL CHILDISH THINGS, then in 2007 for LANGUAGE LESSONS, in 2010 for IT CAME FROM MARS and in 2012 for ALL CHILDISH THINGS. Other plays include SALVAGE, THE GRAVEDIGGER - A FRANKENSTEIN PLAY, NORTHERN AGGRESSION, DR. SEWARD'S DRACULA, INVASIVE SPECIES, THE SCULLERY MAID, NIGHT BLOOMING, and EBENEZER.

POINT OF ORIGIN won Best Locally Created Script 2002 from the Ann Arbor News, and THE STILLNESS BETWEEN BREATHS also won Best New Play 2005 from the Oakland Press. THE STILLNESS BETWEEN BREATHS and IT CAME FROM MARS were selected to appear in the National New Play Network's Festival of New Plays. He also co-authored Flyover, USA: Voices From Men of the Midwest at the Williamston Theatre (Winner of the 2009 Thespie Award for Best New Script). He also adapted CHRISTMAS CAROL'D for the Performance Network.

IT CAME FROM MARS was a recipient of 2009's Edgerton Foundation New American Play Award, and won Best New Script 2010 from the Lansing State Journal. His play ALL CHILDISH THINGS won the Edgerton Foundation New American Play Award in 2011.

Joseph is a founding member of the Roustabout Theatre Company and an Associate Artist at First Folio Shakespeare, an Artistic Ambassador to the National New Play Network, and an adjunct lecturer at Eastern Michigan University, where he teaches Dramatic Composition.

More Plays From SORDELET INK

A Tale of Two Cities
by Christoper M Walsh
adapted from the novel by Charles Dickens

The Count of Monte Cristo
by Christoper M Walsh
adapted from the novel by Alexandre Dumas

The Moonstone
by Robert Kauzlaric
adapted from the novel by Wilkie Collins

Her Majesty's Will
by Robert Kauzlaric
adapted from the novel by David Blixt

Season on the Line
by Shawn Pfautsch
adapted from Herman Melville's Moby-Dick

Action Movie: The Play
by Joe Foust and Richard Ragsdale

Once A Ponzi Time
by Joe Foust

Eve of Ides
by David Blixt

Visit www.sordeletink.com for more!

www.ingramcontent.com/pod-product-compliance
Lightning Source LLC
Chambersburg PA
CBHW070338130626
46556CB00007B/2928